Princess Abby and her sister, Emma, sipped tea in the garden.

Tickle. Tickle.

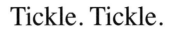

Something tickled Abby's leg.

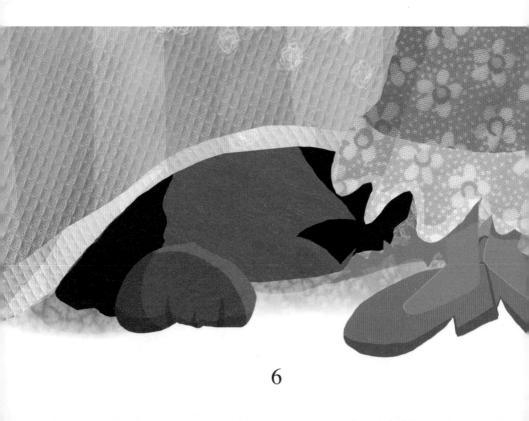

Abby giggled and she wiggled.

Tickle. Tickle.

Abby looked under the table.

Puppy barked and jumped.

"It's not playtime,"

Emma told Puppy.

Tickle. Tickle.

"Shoo." Abby clapped her hands.

Puppy ran out of the garden.

Abby and Emma finished their tea.

Now it was playtime.

"Puppy," Princess Abby called.

"Puppy," called Princess Emma.

Puppy didn't come.

"Maybe Puppy ran up the tower,"
said Abby.

The princesses looked in the tower,

but they didn't find Puppy.

Abby opened the castle door.

"Puppy," she called.

Abby looked in Puppy's bed,

but she didn't find Puppy.

"Puppy," Princess Emma called.

Emma looked in her bedroom,

but she didn't find Puppy.

"Puppy," Princess Abby called.

She looked in the library,

but she didn't find Puppy.

Emma stopped at a closed door.

"What if Puppy is in the basement?"

she asked.

"Puppy," Abby called.

"Woof. Woof," said Puppy.

Princess Abby and Princess Emma

looked into the basement.

"Puppy!" they called.

Puppy didn't come.

"Woof. Woof," said Puppy.

"Puppy needs us," said Abby.

"I'm not going down there,"
Emma said.

Abby was afraid of the dark.

Abby had to be very brave.

"Jesus, help me be brave,"

prayed Abby.

Abby took a lantern.

She tiptoed down the stairs.

Abby's knees shook.

"Jesus is with me," she said.

"Woof. Woof," said Puppy.

Abby found Puppy stuck in a box.

Tickle. Tickle.

Abby tickled Puppy's chin.

"Thank you, Jesus, for making

me brave," prayed Abby.

Abby carried Puppy upstairs.

Puppy woofed and wiggled.

Now it really was playtime.